WITHDRAWN

MANGABOOM

By
Charlotte Pomerantz

Pictures by
Anita Lobel

 Greenwillow Books, New York

Watercolor and gouache paints were used for the full-color art.
The text type is Palatino.
Text copyright © 1997 by Charlotte Pomerantz
Illustrations copyright © 1997 by Anita Lobel

Printed in Singapore by Tien Wah Press
First Edition 10 9 8 7 6 5 4 3 2 1

Library of Congress Cataloging-in-Publication Data
Pomerantz, Charlotte.
Mangaboom / by Charlotte Pomerantz ;
pictures by Anita Lobel.
p.   cm.
Summary: Daniel meets a giant named Mangaboom
who lives in a mango tree and takes him to tea at
her auntie's house.
ISBN 0-688-12956-0 (trade).   ISBN 0-688-12957-9 (lib. bdg.)
[1. Giants—Fiction.]   I. Lobel, Anita, ill.   II. Title.
PZ7.P77Mag   1997   [E]—dc20
96-10416   CIP   AC

for
Carl
Marzani
—C. P.

for
Susan
and
Ava
and
all
my
helpful
friends
at
Greenwillow,
with love
—A. L.

Daniel was walking in the woods when he came to a mango tree. It was the biggest tree he had ever seen. At the bottom was an enormous high-heeled slipper with a satin bow. The slipper was tied with a rope that seemed to rise up and disappear into the middle of the tree.

Daniel scratched his ear. He put one foot in the slipper, then the other. He held onto the rope to steady himself when, all of a sudden, the slipper began to rise into the air.

Looking down he saw two envelopes at his feet. He kept holding the rope with one hand while he picked up the envelopes with the other.

Higher and higher and higher he rose, brushing against leaves and branches and hundreds and hundreds of golden mangoes. Near the top of the tree he landed with a thud on a large wooden platform.

When he looked around, he saw one huge bare foot and one huge slippered foot. Above that was a great billowy dress with flowers, and ruffles at the hem. Still farther up was a smiling face encircled by masses of curly red hair.

"Holy mo," said Daniel. "A lady giant."

"Yes," said a lusty voice. "And you are a young lad who is standing in my slipper. I leave it at the bottom of the tree for letters."

Daniel stepped out and handed her the envelopes. "*Gracias*," said the giant, tucking them into a puffed sleeve. She lowered herself onto a bench, lifted the ruffled hem of her dress, and put on the slipper. Then she held out both feet and admired them.

"Pretty, aren't they?"

Daniel gulped. "Very pretty," he said.

The giant smiled in such a friendly way that Daniel said, "Who are you, please?"

"My name is Mangaboom," she said. "I'm nineteen feet tall and weigh six hundred and eighty-two pounds. I speak Spanish and English. I like to fish and climb trees. I also like to skinny-dip and turn cartwheels on the beach." She paused and said, "I live alone, and my home is here at the top of this mango tree. Now tell me about you."

Daniel sucked in his breath. "My name is Daniel. I'm taller than all my friends. I know a few words in Spanish. I'm here visiting, and last week I caught an octopus."

"*Caramba*!" exclaimed Mangaboom. "With your hands or with a net?"

"A net," said Daniel. "Octopuses are very wriggly."

Just then a goat leaped out of the corner, jumped onto the giant's lap, and began nibbling on the ruffles.

"My pet goat," said Mangaboom.

"I have a rabbit," said Daniel. "She's a foot tall with her ears up. Aren't you going to open your mail?"

"Yes," said Mangaboom. "It looks like a letter from a neighbor, and an invitation from my auntie Tía Pepita asking me to come to a tea party. Whenever Auntie meets an eligible giant, she invites me for tea."

"Eligible?" asked Daniel.

"Someone who might want to marry me," explained Mangaboom.

"I'm never going to get married," said Daniel. "Are you?"

"It depends," said Mangaboom. "The giants I meet at Auntie's house don't interest me." She put on very large spectacles and read,

"'Dear Manguita . . .'"

Mangaboom put the letter down. "Auntie calls me Manguita, which means little mango. She doesn't think Mangaboom is ladylike. Especially the *boom* part."

"The *boom* part is the part I like best," said Daniel.

Mangaboom held up the letter and began again.

"'Dear Manguita,
'I'm having a tea party this afternoon.
I've invited not one, not two, but
three eligible giants. Please come
as soon as you read this.
           'Abrazos de oso,
                         'Auntie'"

"*Abrazos de oso*?" said Daniel.
   "That means hugs of a bear,"
   said Mangaboom.
   "Oh," said Daniel. "Bear hugs." He
   smiled. "Are you going to the tea party?"
   "Sure," said Mangaboom. "I always go
   to Auntie's tea parties." She glanced at
Daniel. "Would you like to come?"
"Would I!" said Daniel. "I've never seen three
   eligible giants."

Mangaboom opened the second letter.
"Mm," she said. "I don't recognize the handwriting."
She read,

"'Dear Lady,
'My name is Grizwaldo. I live in a jacaranda tree. One day, when I went fishing in a nearby stream, I saw you pass by. I had never seen a woman carry herself so straight and tall and proud. Please write. My address is on the envelope.
'Grizwaldo'"

Mangaboom clasped the letter to her giant bosom. "Ay," she said, "my first love letter."
Daniel whistled softly. "Boy, are you lucky. I've never gotten one. Will you answer him?"

"Right away," said Mangaboom, reaching for a pencil
the size of a baseball bat. "Where did I put the envelope
with Grizwaldo's address?"

They looked and looked, but it was nowhere to be
seen. They were staring at one another when they
heard a low *munch-crunch.*

The goat was swallowing the last bit of envelope.
Mangaboom smiled bravely, but Daniel could see
tears in her eyes.

He reached over and patted her hand. "Don't worry,"
he said. "We'll find the jacaranda tree."

"Oh?" said Mangaboom. "Do you know what it looks
like?"

"No," said Daniel. "Don't you?"

Mangaboom moaned softly. "If only I did."

When they arrived at the tea party,
Tía Pepita looked down at Daniel
and up at Mangaboom.
"Meet my friend Daniel," said Mangaboom.
 Auntie held out a giant hand. "Pleased to
 meet you," she said.
"*Mucho gusto*," said Daniel, looking around
 the cave.
 Auntie turned toward Mangaboom.
"Manguita, I don't think a woman of your
 size should wear high heels."
 Mangaboom pulled herself up to her full height.
"Tía Pepita, you might as well face the fact
 that I'm a big woman."
"Big and beautiful," said Daniel.

There were three loud knocks, and three gentleman giants lumbered in and tipped their hats.

"Fee fi fo, hello," they said.

"I'm Tito."

"I'm Fito."

"And I'm Hernando-Fernando. Who's your little friend?"

"His name is Daniel," said Mangaboom. "And he's not little. He's taller than all his friends."

Auntie stepped forward.

"I'm Tía Pepita," she said. "And this is my niece, Manguita."

The giants looked up at Mangaboom and nodded stiffly. They had never met a lady giant who was taller than they were.

"Do you always wear high-heeled slippers?" asked Tito, Fito, and Hernando-Fernando.

"No," said
Mangaboom.
"Only when I
go fishing or tree
climbing or turning
cartwheels on the
beach." She scratched
her nose. "I don't
wear them when I go
skinny-dipping."
The giants turned red.
"S-skinny dipping. You
mean with *n-nada* on?"
they stammered, blushing
and bumping into one another.
"Sure," said Daniel. "It's lots of fun."

They all sat down to tea. Tía Pepita poured.

"Yum," said Tito, biting into a cookie.

"Yum fum," said Fito.

"Yummy fummy," said Hernando-Fernando. "I love your heart-shaped cookies, Auntie."

"Thank you," said Auntie. "But Manguita's cookies are even better."

"What nonsense!" said Mangaboom. "Auntie is the best cookie-maker in the forest."

"Now, Manguita," chided Auntie, "don't be modest."

"Fee fi, I like modest women," said Tito.

"Fi fee, I agree," said Fito.

"Fi fo, it's so," said Hernando-Fernando. "A woman should stay in the house and do what she is told."

Mangaboom glowered at them. "Not in *my* house!" she roared.

"Or anyplace else," said Daniel. "Nobody pushes Mangaboom around. She weighs over six hundred pounds."

"Six hundred and eighty-two, to be exact," said Mangaboom. "And *nobody* tells me what to do."

The giants stared into their teacups and munched on the last of the heart-shaped cookies.

They rose from the table and brushed the cookie
crumbs off their clothing.

"So glad to have met Daniel and your nice niece,"
they said as they bumbled out the door.

"Oh dear," said Tía Pepita, fanning herself
with an elephant-ear fern. "There go three
eligible giants."

Mangaboom threw Auntie a kiss. "Thank
you for the tea," she said.

"*Gracias* for the tea and cookies," said Daniel.
They were halfway out the door when
Mangaboom turned around. "Auntie, have
you ever seen a jacaranda tree?"

"Jacaranda?" said Auntie. "How do you
spell it?"

"J-a-c-a-r-a-n-d-a," said Mangaboom, calling
out each letter.

They could see Tía Pepita rolling the word
on her tongue. There was a long silence.

"No," she said finally.

Outside the cave Mangaboom sighed.
"If only my goat hadn't eaten that
envelope," she said. "Grizwaldo
likes me the way I am."

When they got back to the tree,
only the topmost branches were
tipped with sunlight.

"It's time for me to leave," said Daniel.
"I promised I'd be back before sunset."

"You'll come tomorrow, won't you?" said
Mangaboom.

"*Mañana*," said Daniel. "Of course."

He watched as Mangaboom planted one
slippered foot, then the other, onto branches
that served as a ladder.

Soon all he could see were her flowery dress
and her ruffled hem. Then two high-
heeled slippers with satin bows.
Then nothing.

When Daniel arrived the next day, the giant's slipper was waiting.
He stepped in, and once again there was an envelope at his feet.
He picked it up and turned it over, looking for an address. But
there was none.

He tugged on the rope. Soon he was floating skyward, brushing
against leaves and branches and hundreds and hundreds of golden
mangoes.

When Mangaboom saw him, she called out cheerily, "*Hola*, Daniel,
you're just in time for tea."

A table was set for two. There was a giant teacup, a regular teacup,
and a platter of cookies.

They sat down, and Mangaboom poured.

Daniel blew on his tea to cool it and bit into a cookie.

"Fee fi fo fum," he said. "This little cookie is yum yum yum."

They giggled and winked at each other.

The goat wandered over and began to nibble a few ruffles.

"I forgot to give you this," said Daniel,
   handing the envelope to Mangaboom.
   The goat eyed it hungrily, but Mangaboom
   snatched it and turned it over. Then she sighed,
   put on her spectacles, opened the letter, and read,

"'Dear Lady,
   'I think you will like the cool blue blossoms of my jacaranda
   tree. Perhaps you will like me, too. I will be waiting by your
   tree an hour before sunset.

                              'Grizwaldo'"

Mangaboom held the letter against her heart. "My second love
   letter," she said.
   Through the shiny, pointed leaves of the mango tree, they could
   see the daylight fading all around them.
"It's time for me to start back," said Daniel.
"I know," said Mangaboom. "But I promise to tell you about
   Grizwaldo tomorrow."
"I can't come tomorrow," he said.
"No?" said Mangaboom. "Well, then, the day after."
   Daniel shook his head. "I am leaving tomorrow morning."
   Mangaboom looked at him earnestly. "But surely you'll come
   back some day."
   Daniel looked out at the darkening sky. "Some day," he said.
   The giant handed him a basket with a cloth on top. "Mango
   pops, mango drops, mango creams, mango dreams. Just
   something to remember me by," she said.
"I don't need anything to remember you," said Daniel.
"You are the nicest giant I ever met. And the most
   beautiful."
   Mangaboom's great round eyes grew misty, and her red
   curls and
   ruffles
   trembled.

"My," she said. "What a nice time we have had." She leaned
over, took off her slipper, and attached the rope around it.
Daniel stepped in, holding the basket with one hand and
waving good-bye with the other.

Soon he was being lowered slowly, gently through an airy
forest of branches, shiny leaves, and hundreds and hundreds
of golden mangoes. Down, down, down to the bottom of
the tree. He stepped out and called up, "*Adiós*, Mangaboom . . ."
From the topmost branches the giant's voice answered,
"Good-bye, Daniel . . ."

Daniel had turned and started walking
when he saw a gentleman giant, almost
as tall as Mangaboom, come striding
through the trees.

Daniel stopped and stood very still.
The giant walked up to the mango tree
and waited. In one hand he held two
fishing poles. In the other, a bouquet
of blue blossoms.

Soon a high-heeled slipper poked
out of the tree, followed by a bare
foot, ankles, legs, and a flowery
dress with ruffles. Mangaboom
was descending.

She stepped onto the ground and put on the other slipper.

"Good evening, Grizwaldo," she said. "Have you been waiting for me very long?"

Grizwaldo looked up at her shyly. "All my life," he said.

Mangaboom chuckled softly. "How nice. By the way, have you ever caught an octopus?"

"No," said Grizwaldo.

"Neither have I," said Mangaboom. "But I have a friend who did."

"*Caramba*!" said Grizwaldo. "By hand or with a net?"

"With a net," said Mangaboom. "Octopuses are very wriggly."

Daniel smiled and started back through the woods.

el fin